# Tweak and the Absolutely Right Whale

by Patricia Bell Dubin

Illustrated by Regan

ISBN 1-880812-06-1


Published by Storytellers Ink
Seattle, Washington


Printed in the United States of America

To all the children in my life – young and old, big and small –
who may not feel as good about themselves as they should.

Deep under the ocean and far out to sea
lived a dolphin named Tweak
and his large family:
his brothers and sisters,
his uncles and aunts,
his nieces and nephews,
and grandmas and gramps.

They loved one another
there was rarely a spat;
they cared for each other,
'cause dolphins do that.
But well-meaning love
can be blind, you'll agree,
and poor Tweak was unhappy,
but no one could see.

"You're clever and handsome,"
his mother would say.
But it seemed that young Tweak
didn't see it that way.
He only felt awkward,
alone and apart,
and Tweak was quite certain
he wasn't too smart.

Sea-school for young dolphins
goes on year-around
full of lessons in which work
and play both abound.
As you can imagine
this was hard on poor Tweak
who thought he was stupid,
and school pretty bleak.

But Tweak had a system
that did seem to help.
He would inconspicuously
hide behind kelp.
"If the teacher can't see me,"
reasoned Tweak all along,
"she won't ask me questions
I am bound to get wrong."

This deception worked well
for a very long time,
but then something happened
to put Tweak in a bind.
There were too many pupils.
A bigger classroom would help.
So school moved to a spot
without one speck of kelp.

That day, quite upset,
and not watching his tail,
Tweak—quite literally—
bumped into a whale.
The whale was so startled
he let go a spout
that hurtled Tweak airborne,
dorsal fin over snout.

Once Tweak had landed
still scared but polite,
he swam to apologize
(mom had brought him up right).
"I can't tell you, Your Whaleship,
how sorry I am.
From now on I'll be careful—
it won't happen again."

The whale laughed a whale laugh (he was not at all mean),
and he grinned a whale grin full of shiny baleen.
"Not to worry young man, what's your name?" (Tweak said "Tweak")
"I've collided with worse any day of the week."

"Just the same," Tweak announced, "you must think I am nuts.
You don't broadside a whale 'less you're really a klutz!"
"Hmmm," answered the whale, "son, come here, close to my eye.
I detect discontent, and I'd like to see why."

Tweak, following orders, took the long way around
to examine the whale from both upside and down.
"I've seen many a whale," he announced to the eye,
"but recall none like you—and that's surely no lie."

The eye seemed to twinkle (is that likely at all?)
and the whale answered Tweak in his foreign whale drawl.
"That makes perfect sense because I'm not from here,
but I like to vacation this time of the year."

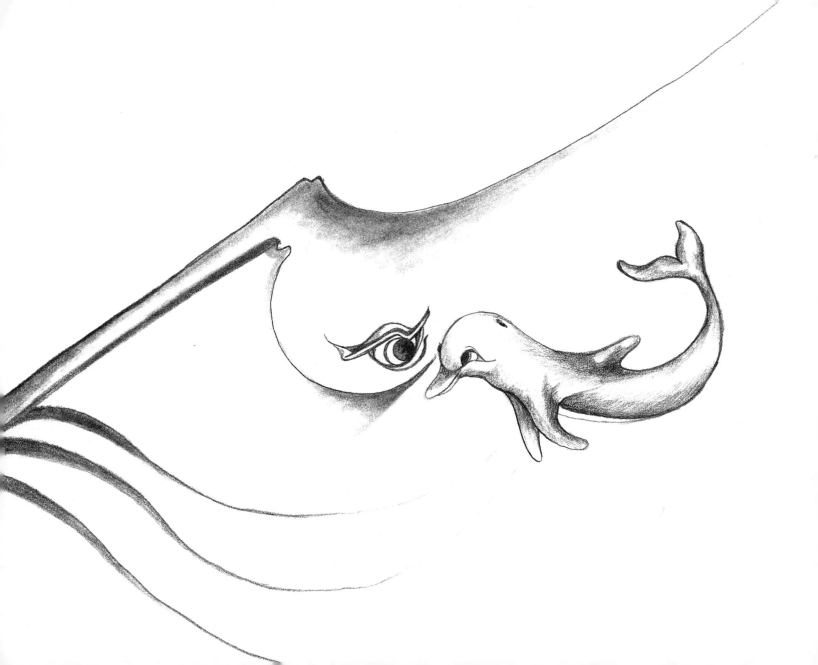

"I am called a *right* whale
by the mammals on land,
so I go by that name
'cause I think it's quite grand."
Tweak, suddenly awestruck,
eyes starting to blink,
repeated, "A *right* whale—
does that mean what I think?"

"Oh, I doubt it," the whale laughed
(this whale liked to tease),
and I want to discuss it,
but I do have to breathe!"
So they both broke the surface,
each exhaling a spout,
the whale's tall and whale-like,
Tweak's smaller, no doubt.

Now Tweak was intrigued,
as they started to swim—
a *right* whale, he pondered—
then pondered again.
"If I pose a question,"
he asked from the tail,
"will you always be right?"
"Of course!" claimed the whale.

9

Tweak spun 'round in the air
and stood up on his tail,
turned a back somersault,
then followed the whale.
"I am not very bright,
I don't do well in school.
Could you help with my homework
so I don't look like a fool?"

"Is it too much to ask?
Am I way out of line?
I don't want to look dumb
so I'm scared all the time."
And when Tweak stopped talking,
he looked worried and small.
"I will," said the whale.
"It's no trouble at all."

From that moment forward
their friendship would start,
and right whale and dolphin
were never apart.
Each day after school
when Tweak met his new chum
they'd discuss what Tweak learned
and that made it more fun.

If the homework, let's say,
was a shipwreck or boat,
they'd seek out examples
both sunk and afloat.
They'd study and explore,
puzzle and explain
while data was stored
in Tweak's over-sized brain.

The whale did not say much
 —surprising to hear—
but listened intently,
and sometimes would steer.
They reviewed the assignments
before Tweak went to bed,
and when Tweak gave right answers,
"Absolutely!" Right said.

Because Tweak thought this whale
was the smartest he'd known,
he gave the whale credit
for successes his own.
There were other improvements—
Tweak began to like school.
He would volunteer answers
without feeling a fool.

One day Tweak and the whale had just taken a dive,
and were feeling elated just being alive
when the sound of loud engines was heard overhead,
and then for some reason Tweak experienced dread.

Tweak didn't have time to ask what "dread" meant,
when his whole life was altered by one horrid event.
Just a second elapsed from the sound of a splash
when a huge metal thing hit the whale with a crash.

The force of the impact sent the whale spinning 'round;
the weight of the anchor pushed his mighty bulk down.
Tweak darted around him (he was shaking with fright),
and he just kept repeating, "Sir, are you all right?"

With the last of his strength, when Tweak asked what to do,
the whale gasped, "Can't help now—it's all up to you."
And with those final words, perhaps facing death's door,
the whale fell unconscious on the deep ocean floor.

"No, wake up, Mr. Right!"
Tweak started to wail,
as he slapped the whale's nose
with his vibrating tail.
"Please don't leave me alone–
I don't know what to do.
When I've dealt with these problems
I've always asked you."

But the whale remained still,
and his eyes remained closed.
He offered no answers
to the questions Tweak posed.
Some minutes were wasted
while Tweak couldn't stir,
till suddenly he saw
just how precious they were.

A whale has to breathe
each half-hour, more or less;
how much time had been wasted
Tweak tried not to guess.
There's no time to feel sorry,
and no time to be scared
for when a friend needs you,
you must be prepared.

Tweak swam in a circle
as fast as he could,
until his mind cleared
as he hoped that it would.
Then Tweak sent out a message
by sonar-type thought
to inform all his friends
of the help that he sought.

22

Well, it took only seconds
for word to get through,
and within minutes, at most,
there assembled a crew.
Tweak's large dolphin family
all showed up in force
with whales, seals and swordfish—
and octopi, of course.

They all saw the problem
(it was clearly at hand),
and they swam around shouting,
each taking command.
The seals barked out orders,
dolphins analyzed the plight
while whales pushed the anchor
with considerable might.

The swordfish tried sawing
their way through the chain,
the octopi pulled with each
leg, but in vain.
Tweak studied the anchor,
and followed the chain.
"I must find," he reasoned,
"the source of this pain."

He remembered his lessons,
and applied what he'd learned.
A cruise ship, he figured,
as he swam, bow to stern.
It was very impressive
–so big and so tall–
beside it, this dolphin
felt awfully small.

The boat contained humans;
Tweak saw heads here and there.
And whenever they saw him
they started to stare.
"It's simple," thought Tweak,
"I'll explain, and they'll leave."
So he started to talk
and he started to plead.

Though Tweak's plea meant nothing
it still made a hit,
and as more came to watch
the ship tilted a bit.
Tweak thought for a minute,
then suddenly knew.
He dove with a vengeance
and instructed his crew.

"All right, pay attention!
Listen up, and be fast!"
And they all stopped and looked at him,
slightly aghast.
Was this really our Tweak?
(Their eyes grew quite large.)
But it was little Tweak
and completely in charge!

"You swordfish, go quickly
and bring back some kelp.
You octopi tie it
'round the whale like a belt.
The strongest of fishes
use your fins to the hilt
to push hard on the anchor
when the boat starts to tilt."

He turned to the others:
"We must jump and cavort–
and do it together,
first starboard, then port.
When everyone's watching
our tricks and our craft,
we'll switch and perform them
first forward, then aft."

They were stunned for a minute,
(had Tweak cracked from the strain?)
but Tweak hadn't the patience
or time to explain.
"You must trust me," he said,
(and you know they all did)
so they broke off and scattered
to do as he bid.

Well, you'd never believe
what transpired after that:
an incredible show
of marine acrobats.
Dolphins spun and they flipped,
clicked and whistled and squealed.
The whales breached and spy-hopped,
and they fluked and they wheeled.

Seals barked and applauded
as they swam upside-down,
and the sailfish and marlin
seemed to fly all around.
They would suddenly vanish
as if to hide,
only to surface again
on the opposite side.

The boat took to rocking
starboard, port, bow and stern.
And the fast-shifting anchor
made the sea start to churn.
The ship was in chaos,
all you heard were the cries,
for it looked in a moment
like the boat would capsize.

Then all of a sudden
the show came to a stop.
It turned so still and quiet
you could hear a fish flop.
The humans stood silent
and looked nervously down,
because from somewhere below
came an ominous sound.

A gurgle of bubbles, a "blurp" then a "glop."
A strange "slick" or "footprint" emerged at the top.
Next came a rumble which progressed to a scream,
as a whale burst through the water like a huge submarine.

Each human in concert said "Aaah!" and then "Ooooh!"
As the whale hit the surface he literally flew.
Then he spouted so high a whale record was set;
when he belly-flopped down he got everyone wet.

He rested a minute, buoyed up by the kelp,
then he wriggled it off without anyone's help.
He turned on his side, fixed the boat with his eye,
then rolled, waved a flipper, and fluked a "Goodbye!"

And what of the humans? I'd be willing to say
not one would forget the events of that day.
While those in the water were having great fun
Tweak's family delighted in all he had done.

"That's my boy," said his mom. (Can a dolphin blush red?)
"He's as smart as they come, that's what I've always said!"
Shy Tweak mumbled, "Anyone would have known what to do."
But the whale winked and said, "The one who did it was you!"

And the party continued past high and low tide,
and when it wound down Right took Tweak aside.
"I owe you my life, and I want you to see
what you did was quite clever—and you didn't need me!"

"Look around," the whale said, "such respect you have earned.
I feel confident now of the lessons you've learned."
There was silence a minute (which seemed like a day),
it was clear that the whale had some more left to say.

"I'm afraid," sighed the whale, "for some time I have known
it is getting too warm here, and it's time to go home.
It was just a vacation we both knew from the start.
I stayed longer, you see, 'cause you tugged at my heart."

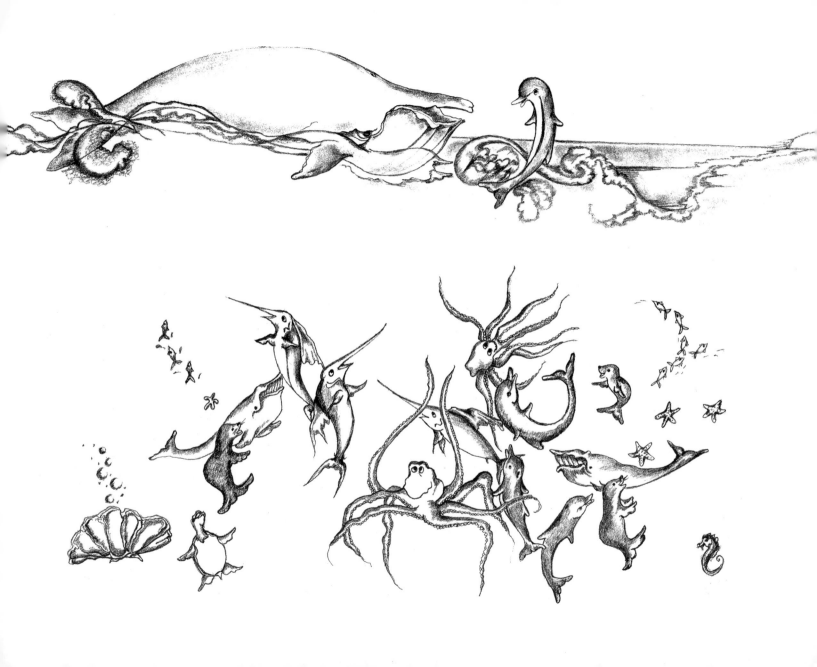

Tweak, clearly upset,
wiped a tear from his eye
(it isn't quite proper
for dolphins to cry).
"Of course, Mr. Right,
do what you must do.
But I'll miss you so much
I won't know what to do."

"You'll be fine," said the whale.
Tweak tried hard to grin
when he felt a definite tug
or two on his fin.
Displeased by the timing
he turned with a grunt
and came face-to-face
with a seal they call Runt.

"Excuse me, Your Tweakship,"
said the seal. "It's just me.
But I'm needing your help
with a problem or three."
Tweak was taken aback,
but he shrugged an O.K.,
and he smiled to himself
at what Runt had to say.

"Gosh, I wish I could be
just as clever as you,
but how not to be dumb,
well, I haven't a clue.
And I feel so alone,
yet I know that's not true,
but I really need help
so I'm turning to you."

"All the help that you need
is inside, be aware.
If you're quiet and listen
the answers are there.
And when you feel abandoned
and left on your own,
if you dig deep inside
you will not be alone."

Tweak turned 'round by habit
for a nod from the whale,
but he had headed for home
with a thrust of his tail.
Though his mighty whale torso
was barely in sight,
his last words rang clearly,
"Absolutely, you're right!"